Sweet Dreams

to a special little girl

with love from

Helga

Sweet
Dreams
5
Minute
Bedtime
Stories

CONTENTS

MARGRET & H.A. REY'S

Sweet Dreams, Curious George

Written by Cynthia Platt

illustrated in the style of H. A. Rey *by* Mary O'Keefe Young

To Barbara and Doc, with love — C.P.

For my sweet dreamers — Bridget, Matt, Tara, and Autumn — M.O'K.Y.

This is George. George is a good little monkey and always very curious.

Today, he's curious about a library book that his friend the man with the yellow hat brought home.

George sat down to look at the book. There was a yellow chick on the cover, pointing up to the sky. This made George even more curious.

He brought it to the
man with the yellow hat.

"Why don't we wait until after dinner, George?" asked his friend. "Then we can read it as a bedtime story."

George wanted to read the book . . . but he was feeling hungry and dinner did smell delicious.

After dinner, it was bathtime. A nice warm bath is just what a monkey needs after a long day! George played with his rubber ducky and little toy boat until it was time to get out.

His friend held out a fluffy towel with a hood that looked like a chick.

That made George think of his new library book!

George put on his pajamas and hopped into bed. He couldn't wait to hear that story!

"This is the story of Chicken Little," said the man with the yellow hat. "I think you're going to like this one, George!"

George did like it! Poor Chicken Little thought the sky was going to fall, and then lots of other animals thought it would too. Thank goodness, the sky didn't actually fall. Little monkeys like happy endings.

It seemed like the perfect bedtime story . . .

That is, until George woke up in the middle of the night! He had had a terrible dream that the sky really was falling.

George was scared.

His friend came to see what was the matter. George pointed to the book and then to the ceiling.

"Don't worry, George—it was just a dream," said his friend. "The sky isn't really going to fall. Let's try to relax and get back to sleep."

First, the man with the yellow hat brought him a cup of warm milk. "Warm milk always makes me feel sleepy, George."

It seemed to be working for George, too, until—oh, no!—the warm milk spilled all over the place.

“Maybe a song will help,” said the man with the yellow hat. “Lie down in bed and I’ll sing to you.”

George tried to rest. He really did. But the song was pretty catchy. First he tapped his toes slowly. Then his whole body wanted to dance!

He got up and bounced on the bed.

“Hmm,” said his friend. “I wish I knew why you can’t sleep tonight!”

George stopped dancing. He pulled out the book *Chicken Little* and then pointed to the ceiling again, frowning.

“Are you still worried that the sky is going to fall?” his friend asked. George nodded. He just couldn’t get that dream out of his head.

“Hmm . . .” said his friend. “I have an idea. Why don’t we take my telescope outside to look at the stars and make sure the sky is still way up where it should be?”

George liked that idea so much that he leaped right out of his bed.

It was chilly outside, but it was very nice to be out in the dark of the night, too. The stars were still up in the sky, far, far away.

The man with yellow hat set up the telescope and showed George how to look through it.

When George looked through the telescope, the stars looked quite near. He could even see planets!

Near . . . far . . . near . . . far. He looked through the telescope many times. It was like magic.

"See, George?" asked his friend. "The stars are just where they should be. That sky doesn't look like it's falling, does it?"
George shook his head with a smile.

The man with the yellow hat even had a chart with something called constellations on them—pictures in the stars!

George loved looking for the constellations so much that he completely forgot about his bad dream.

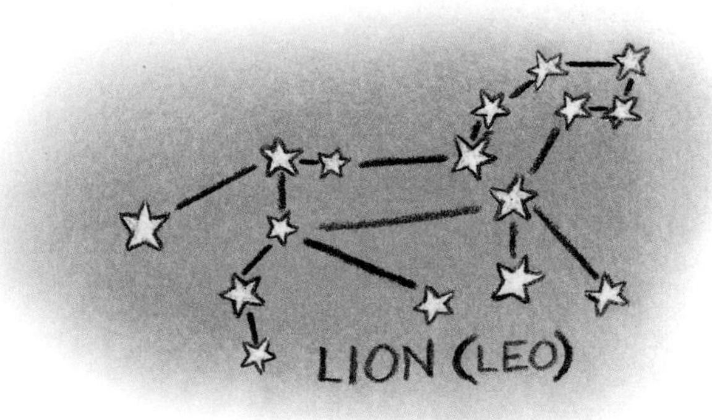

But it was so late! George yawned.

"I think it's time for both of us to get to sleep, George," said his friend, leading him back into the house.

By the time they got back to George's room, he was very tired.

His friend gave him a hug and tucked him in tightly.

"Good night, George," said the man with the yellow hat as he was about to close the door. "I hope you have happy dreams."

As the starlight streamed into his bedroom, George snuggled down deep into his blankets and fell asleep.

Sweet dreams, George!

I WILL NOT READ THIS BOOK

by CECE MENG Illustrated by JOY ANG

To Alex —C.M.

To Mom, Dad, and Josh for your constant support —J.A.

WAIT. BEFORE I READ THIS BOOK,

I have to floss my teeth and wash behind my ears and feed my fish.

WAIT.

Before I read this book,

I have to sip some water

and scratch the tip of my nose

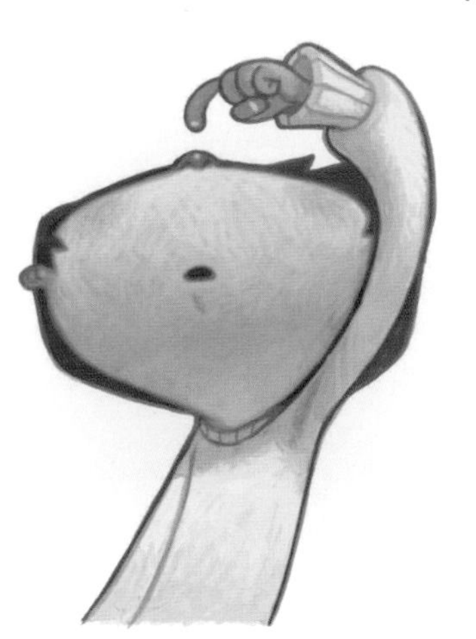

and clean under my bed.

WAIT.

I changed my mind. I am not going to read today. Reading is hard and I don't read fast and sometimes there are words I don't know. I will not read this book and . . .

YOU CAN'T MAKE ME.

I will not read this book even if you hang me upside down . . .

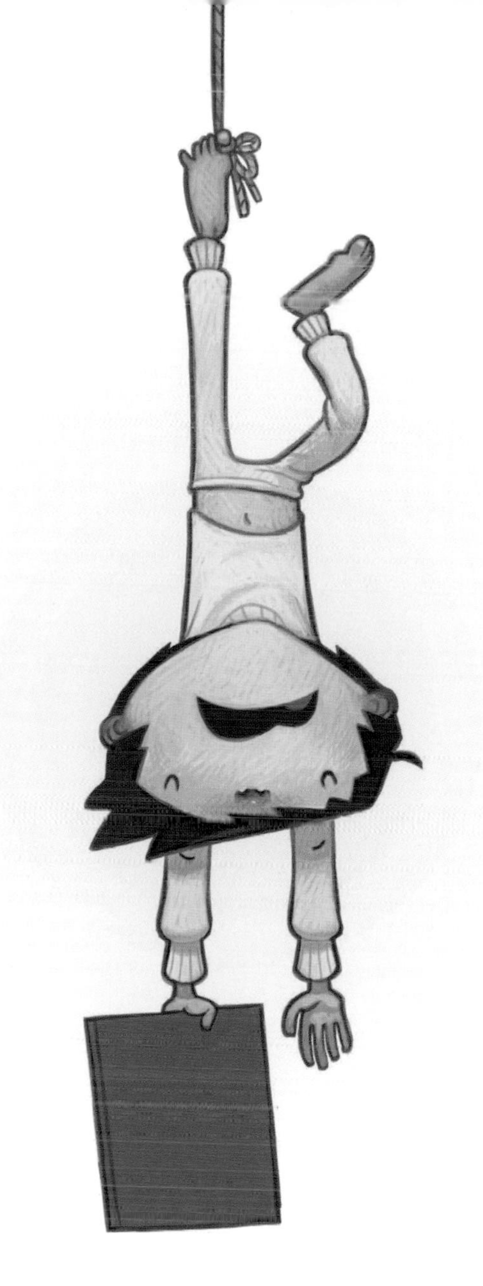

by one toe.

I will not read this book
even if you hang me upside down
by one toe . . .

over a cliff.

I will not read this book
even if you hang me upside down
by one toe
over a cliff . . .

while tickling my feet.

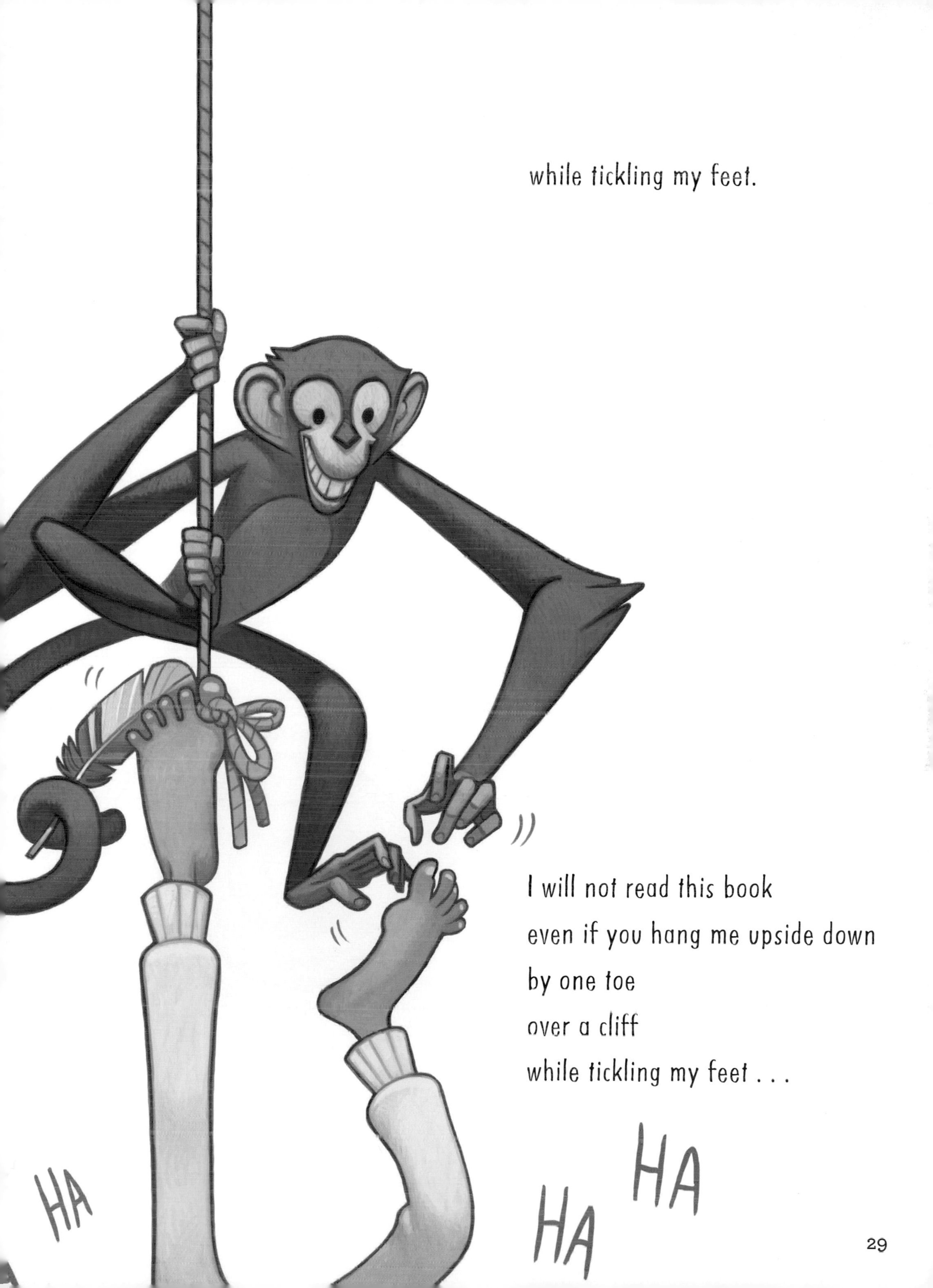

I will not read this book
even if you hang me upside down
by one toe
over a cliff
while tickling my feet . . .

in a rainstorm.

I will not read this book
even if you hang me upside down
by one toe
over a cliff
while tickling my feet
in a rainstorm . . .

with lightning above . . .

and sharks down below.

I will not read this book
even if you hang me upside down
by one toe
over a cliff
while tickling my feet
in a rainstorm
with lightning above
and sharks down below and . . .

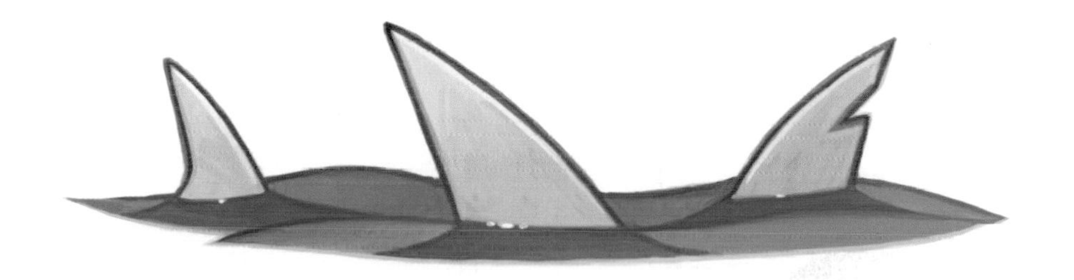

a dragon comes along
and blows smoke in my eyeballs.

I will not read this book
even if you hang me upside down
by one toe
over a cliff
while tickling my feet
in a rainstorm
with lightning above
and sharks down below
and a dragon comes along
and blows smoke in my eyeballs and . . .

all the while there's a
speeding train coming toward us and . . .

I have to sneeze.

I will not read this book
even if you hang me upside down
by one toe
over a cliff
while tickling my feet
in a rainstorm
with lightning above
and sharks down below
and a dragon comes along and
blows smoke in my eyeballs
and all the while there's a
speeding train coming toward us
and I sneeze and . . .

YOU DROP ME!
WAIT.

If you drop me, I might
change my mind and read.

But only if you catch me.

Then I will read this book with you.

GO TO BED, MONSTER!

Written by Natasha Wing

Illustrated by Sylvie Kantorovitz

To the creative monster within—may you never go to sleep.
—N.W.

To Samantha, my drawing monster. With love.
— S.K.

One night, Lucy tossed and turned.
She could not, would not, did not
want to go to bed.
"I want to draw," she said.

Lucy dumped out her crayons. She drew an oval body. A square head. Rectangle legs. And circle eyes.

When she added triangles,
the shapes
turned into a . . .

MONSTER!

said Monster.

"You don't scare me," said Lucy.
"Let's play!"

Lucy and Monster built castles.

They marched in a parade.

Then they skipped

and jumped

until Lucy was
all worn out.

"Let's play sleeping lions,"
said Lucy.

CHASE!

roared Monster.

"I'm too tired," said Lucy.
"And so are you.
Go to bed."

Lucy drew Monster a bed.
But Monster would not go to bed.

roared Monster.

Lucy drew a mountain of meatballs.

Lucy drew a
bucket of water.

Lucy drew a bathroom door.

asked Monster.

"Go to bed," moaned Lucy.

But Monster would not go to bed.

COLD
whined Monster.
Lucy drew pajamas.
SCARED
Lucy drew a huggy bear.

Lucy drew a moon.

Then Lucy crossed her arms.
"That's enough. Now go to bed."

snapped Monster.

"Maybe this will help,"
said Lucy.

BOOK!

cheered Monster.

"Only if you get into bed," said Lucy.

Monster climbed into bed.

sighed Monster.

Lucy tucked in Monster.
Then she read and read and read.

SLEEPY

whispered Monster.

Lucy watched one circle eye,
then two circle eyes, slowly close.

She laid down her head.

Then she finally,

peacefully,

went to sleep.

Joanne Ryder Melissa Sweet

Won't You Be My Hugaroo?

For Larry, my hugaroo . . . and my kissaroo, too. —J.R.

For Rebecca and Evan. —M.S.

Won't you be my *hugaroo*?

I've lots of hugs to share with you.

A catch-you hug is full of play,
although it takes your breath away.

A twirly hug will make you spin
and lift you up until you grin.

A friendly hug is nice and plain.
It's good to be with you again.
A baby hug is sweet and tight
and ends with giggles of delight.

An off-we-go hug can be fun.

Squeeze in tight . . . and here you come!

A tickle hug will make you jiggle
and laugh and squeal
and squirm and wiggle.

A cheer-up hug can save the day
when everything is not okay.

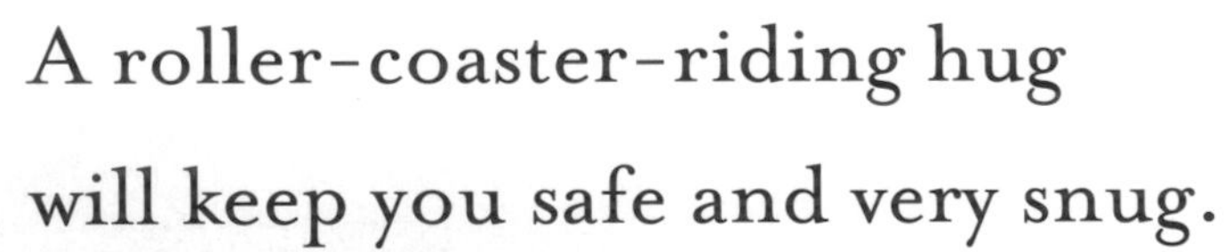

A roller-coaster-riding hug
will keep you safe and very snug.

YOU MUST
TO

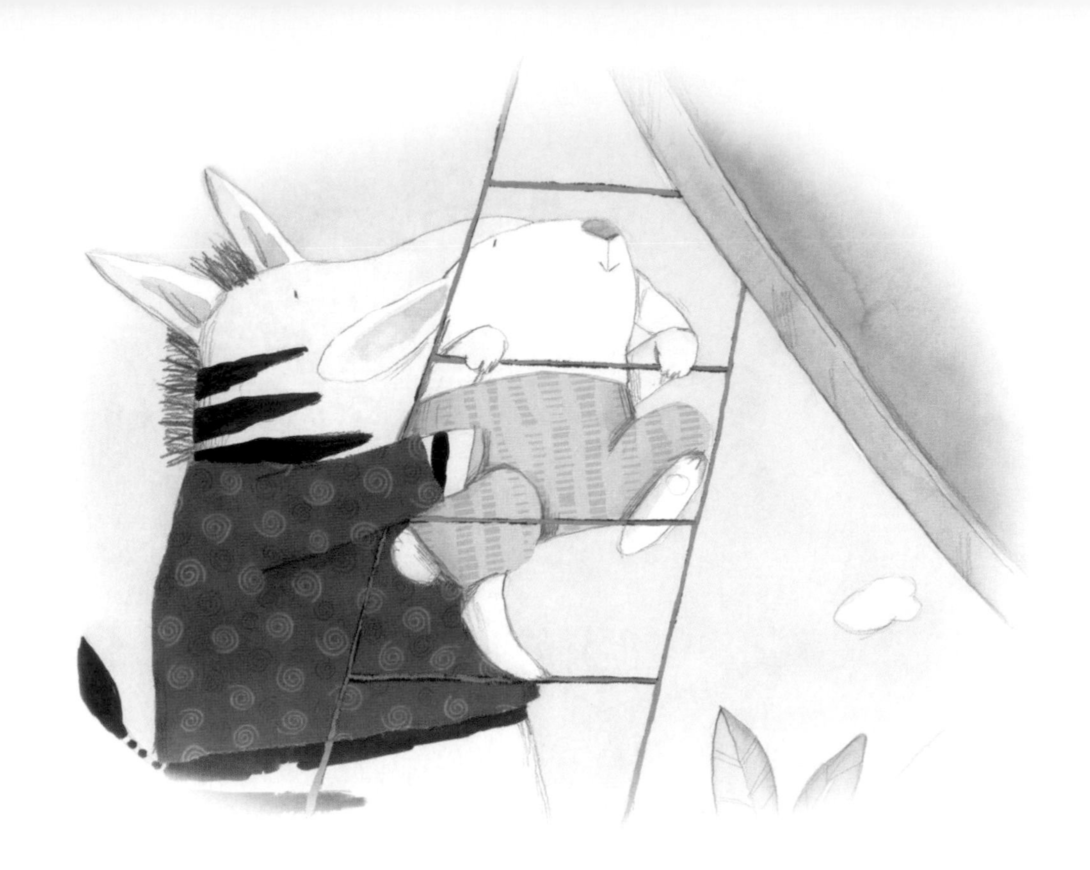

A calming hug will see you through
when something scary frightens you.

A good-job hug makes you feel great.
You've done so well. Let's celebrate!

A cuddly hug on someone's lap
will often end up with a nap.

POPCORN

A good-bye hug is long and slow
'cause no one really wants to go.

A cozy hug when tales are read
is nice to share upon a bed.

So won't you be my *hugaroo*?
And every day, the whole day through,
we'll be as happy as can be . . .

. . . as I hug you and you hug me.

Charlotte Jane Battles Bedtime

Myra Wolfe

illustrated by Maria Monescillo

For my wildly delightful children:
Sophie, James, and Theodore
—M.W.

for Noa, who was born at the same
time as this story's art
—M.M.

CHARLOTTE JANE THE HEARTY came howling into the world with the sunrise.

"Arr. She's finer than a ship full of jewels," said her mother, smiling.

"Arr," agreed her father.

"Also," said her mother, "she's got oomph."

"*Formidable* oomph," said her father.

They were right.
Her first words came early.

Her first steps came late.

She relished swashbuckling sessions,

treasure hunts,

and Fantastic Feats of Daring.

"I like to get all the
juice out of my days!"
she would say.

And bedtime was not juicy.
"Sleep is your friend, little doubloon," said her father.
"No one can be hearty without it," said her mother.
Charlotte Jane did not agree.

She began to go to bed later . . . and later . . .

and later . . .

until one dark night she didn't go to bed at all.

"Victory!" she whispered into the morning.

But Charlotte Jane did not feel hearty.
Her oomph seemed to have gone to
sleep without her.
"Traitor," she said. "A good plate
of cackle fruit will jostle you up."
It didn't.

Neither did a
swashbuckling session
with One-Eyed Tom.

Or a treasure hunt.

And she was too sapped to even think of Fantastic Feats of Daring.

Her parents were worried.
"What's the matter?" asked her mother.
"Aye, sweet pomegranate, tell us," said her father.
"Arr," said Charlotte Jane. "My oomph's weighed anchor."

This would not do.
A hunt for the missing oomph began.

“It’s not in the closet,”
said her mother.

“It’s not in the bathtub!”
called her father.

"It's not in the fridge!"
her mother shouted.

"It's not in the garden!"
her father bellowed.

Charlotte Jane dragged herself up to her room and looked out the window.

There was her mother,
digging through
the neighbor's recycling bin.
There was her father,
climbing the old oak tree.

And there was her featherbed.
Charlotte Jane gave it a fearsome glare.
Bedtime was not juicy. Sleep was for landlubbers.

But dreams . . .

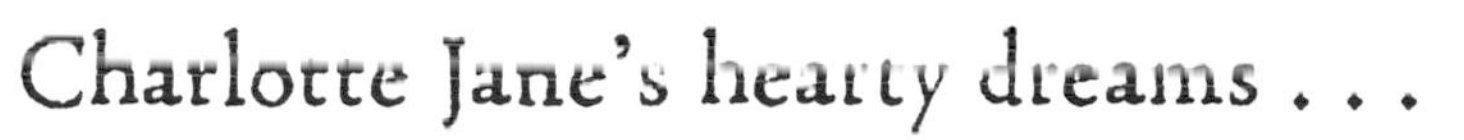

Charlotte Jane's hearty dreams . . .

were rip-roarers!

As the sun came up,
Charlotte Jane
rubbed her eyes.
"Well, blow me down!"

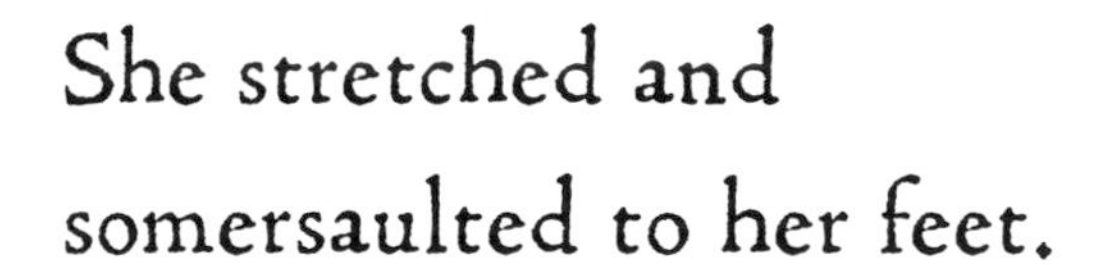

She stretched and
somersaulted to her feet.

"Gangway!" she said.

Charlotte Jane peeked in at her parents.
"Juicy sweet dreams, me buckos," she whispered.
It was time to shiver some timbers.

Charlotte Jane the Hearty's *formidable* oomph was back at last.

Blanket

written and illustrated by MARGOT APPLE

For Elizabeth Doggage and Kitty Lint
and my dear Mr. Smith, whose blanket
cured toothaches
— M.A.

Today we washed Blanket and hung it out to dry.
Mom said that it had to be done.
All day I worried.

When it was time for bed, Blanket was still wet.
Mom said, "Can't take a wet Blanket to bed."
"But how will I sleep?" I asked.

Mom put Ted and Nini and Kitty in bed with me.
First she read us a story, then
she tucked us in and gave me a kiss.
"You can see Blanket out the window," she said,
"and Kitty will help you go to sleep."

My stomach hurt and I could not sleep.
The pillow had lumps and the sheets were cold.
I hugged Kitty tight but she wouldn't hold still.
Blanket was still outside.

Outside it was getting dark.
Blanket sagged and drooped.
Little drops fell from its corners.
"Poor Blanket," said the clothes.

"Poor Blanket," sighed the wind.
"Poor?" said the moon, peeking through the trees.
"Yes, yes, yes . . . Poor, poor, poor!" chirped the bugs.
"We will help you, Blanket," whispered the clothes.
"Wind," they squeaked, "give us a push!"
And the wind answered,
"Wooo . . . pussh. I like to pusshhh!"

"Whisssh . . . weee-ooohh . . . whooossh." The wind pushed.
"Clap, clap, clap . . . Pop, pop, pop." The clothes tugged.
But the window was still too far away.

“Dog,” they all cried, “please, help!”
“Mmnf!” Dog said, jumping on the clothesline.
Back and forth they swung, closer and closer.

Outside I heard little voices saying,
"Reach, Blanket! Stretch, Blanket!"
Kitty wiggled and wiggled.
"Don't go!" I said.
"Ssss-something's wrrrong!" Kitty hissed.
And then *WHAPP*. Blanket hung on the windowsill.
Kitty grabbed it and hung on.

"It's Blanket!" I cried.
"Hold on tight!" called the clothes.
"Amnf," said Dog, "don't let go!"

So I pulled and Kitty pulled.
The clothes worked and worked.
The wind huffed and puffed.

All at once there was a tremendous *HOOOSSH*.

Kitty and I went flying through the air.
“Woo!” cheered the clothes.

The clothes were singing,
"The Blanket's free! The Blanket's free!"

And then they all began to dance.

“Goodnight, clothes and wind and moon,”
we said at last.
“And thank you all very much.”

In the morning, Mom said,
“How did Blanket get inside?
I left it on the clothesline last night.
And, Dog, what are you doing on the bed?”
Kitty smiled and Dog just wagged her tail.

Very Hairy Bear

Alice Schertle

Illustrated by Matt Phelan

To Jen and Drew
John and Kate
Spence and Dylan
—A.S.

For Rebecca
—M.P.

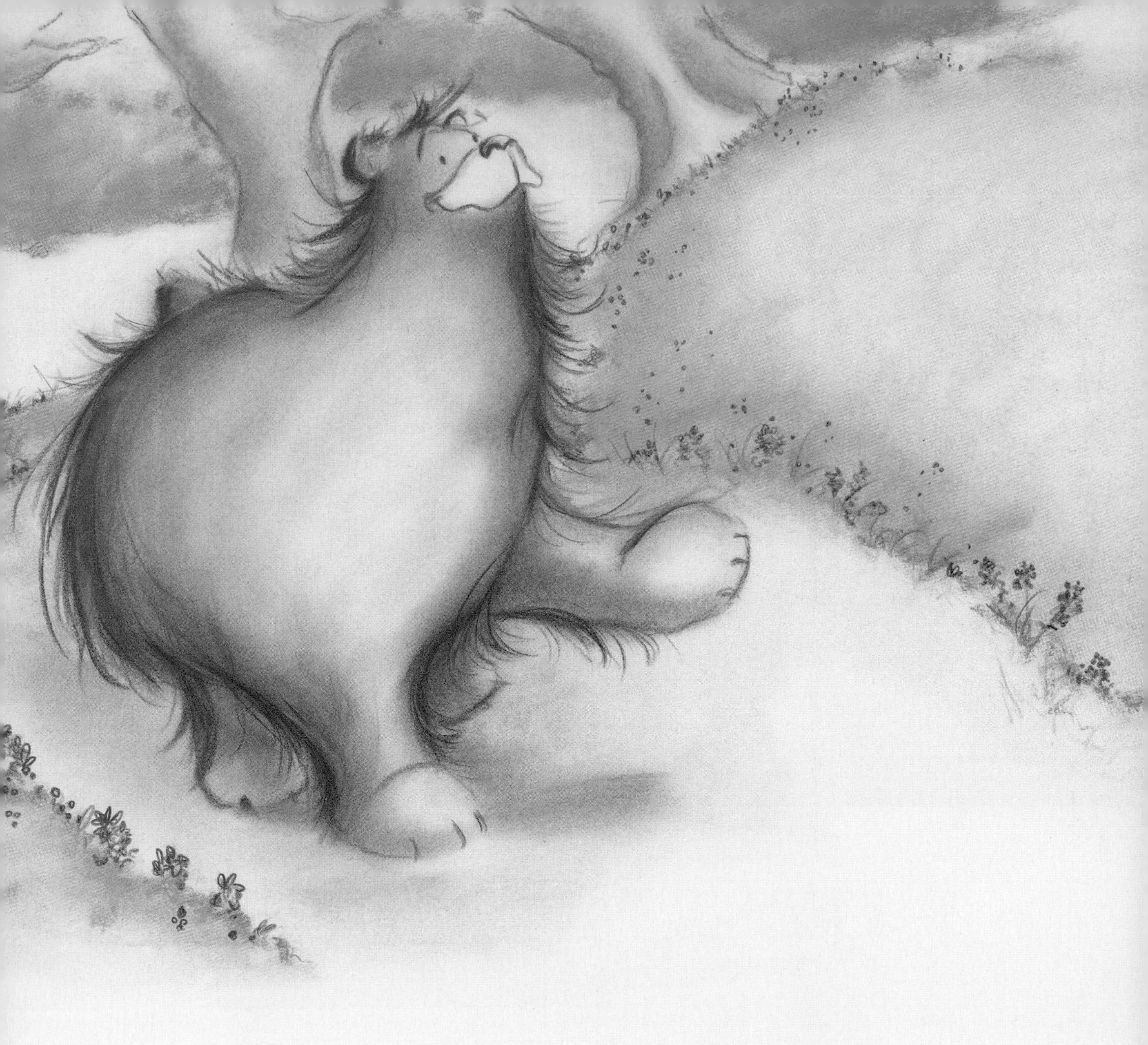

Deep in the green gorgeous wood
lives a boulder-big bear
with shaggy, raggy, brownbear hair
everywhere . . .

except on his no-hair nose.

Each spring,
when the silver salmon leap into the air,
fisherbear is there
to catch them.

He stands in the river
with his brown coat dripping.

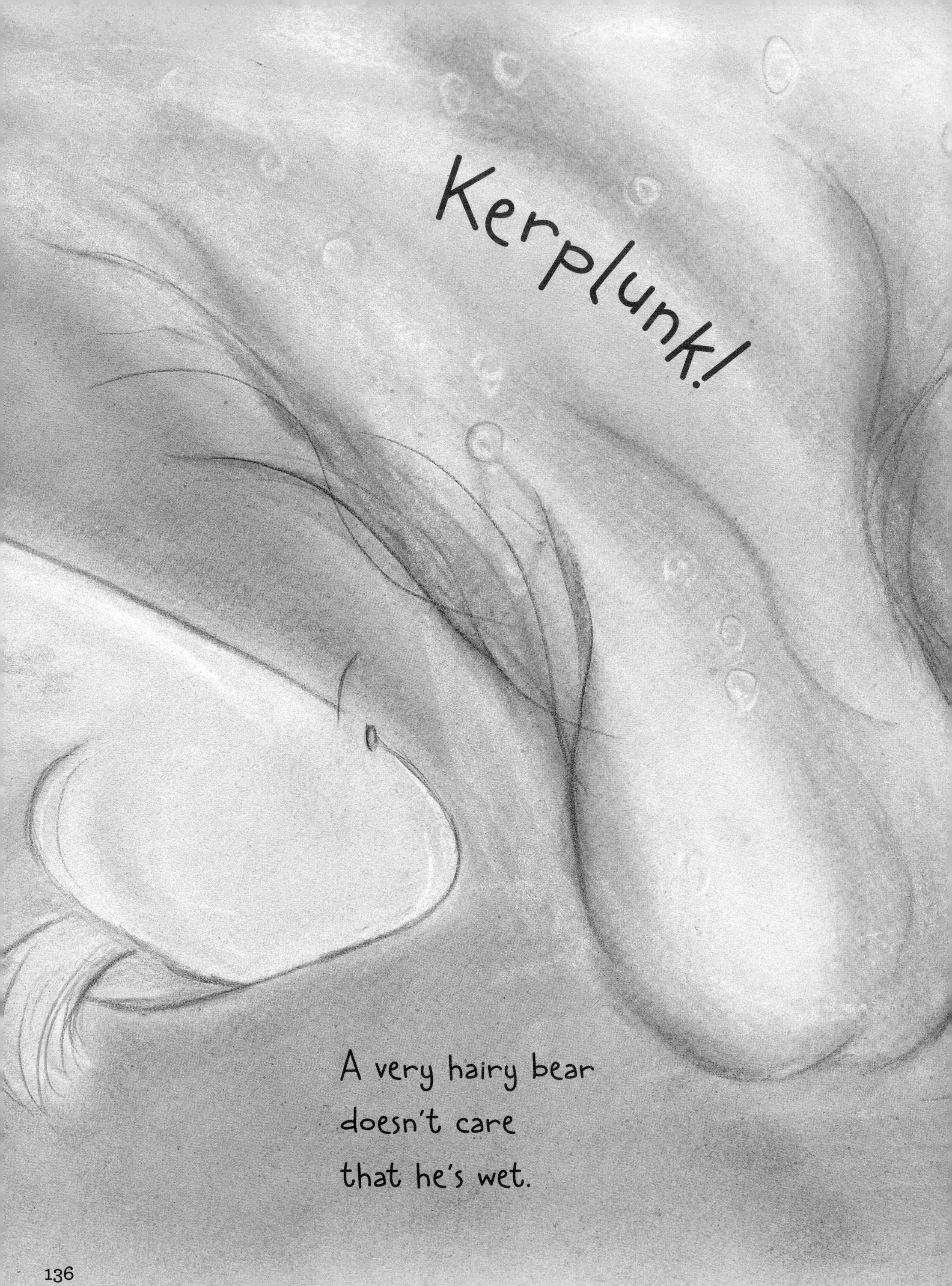

Kerplunk!

A very hairy bear
doesn't care
that he's wet.

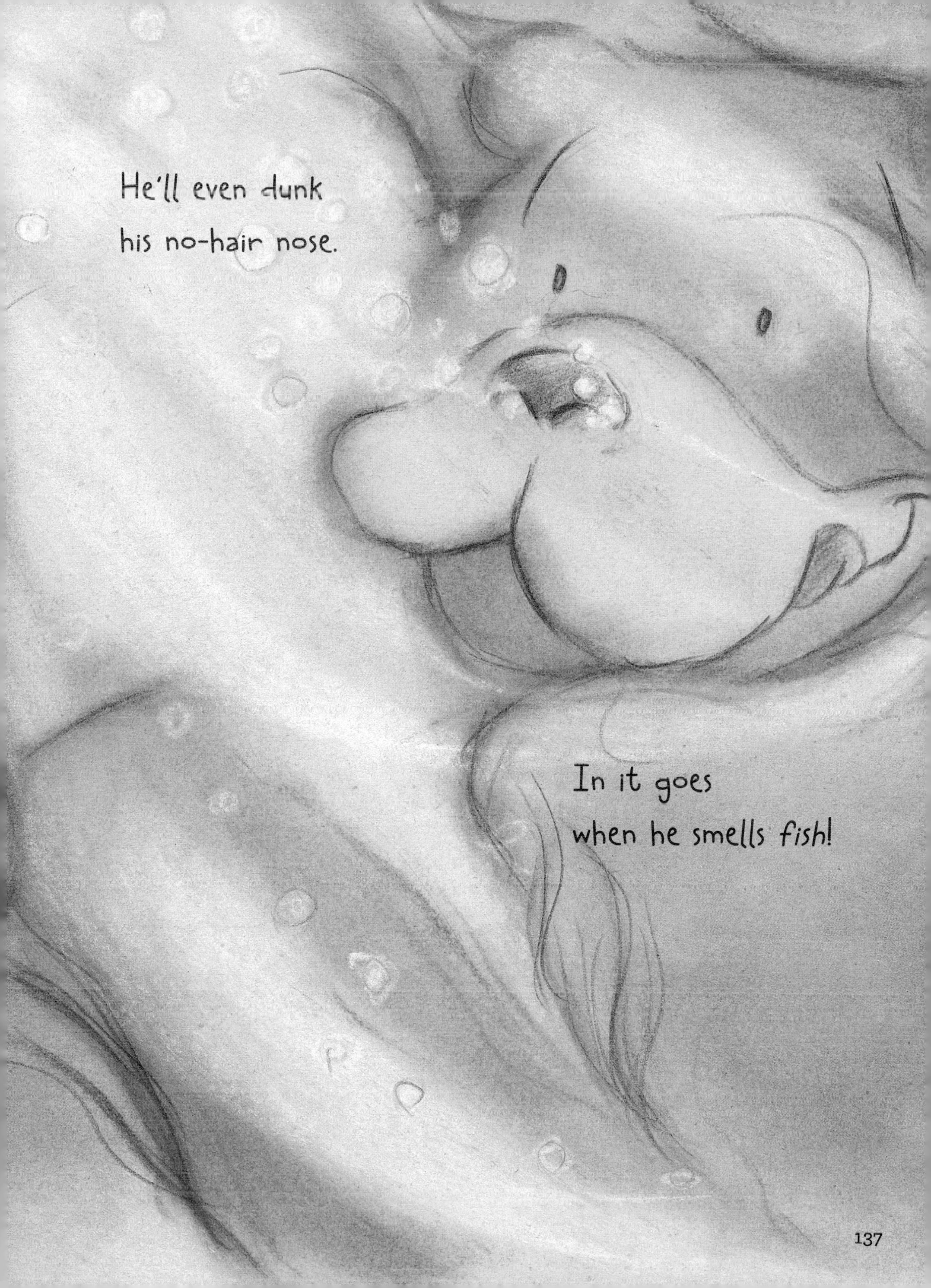

He'll even dunk
his no-hair nose.

In it goes
when he smells *fish*!

Each summer,
he's a sticky, licky honey hunter,
with his bare nose deep
in the hollow of
a bee tree.

A very hairy bear
doesn't care
about stings and things.

Even on his no-hair nose.

When the summer blueberries
grow round and fat on their bushes,
a very hairy bear
doesn't care
that his nose gets blue.

He eats the berries and the bushes, too.
He's a very full
berryfull bear.

In the fall,
when quick gray squirrels hide acorns
under the oak trees,
a no-hair nose knows
where to find them.

A very hairy bear
doesn't care
if the squirrels scold.

He eats all the acorns
he can hold.

Then,

when soft white snowflakes start to fall
and cling to bear hair . . .

(if there's a bear there),

when fish sink to sleep deep in the pond,
wrapped in their silver scales,

and swarms of bees sleep
deep in their warm honey hives,

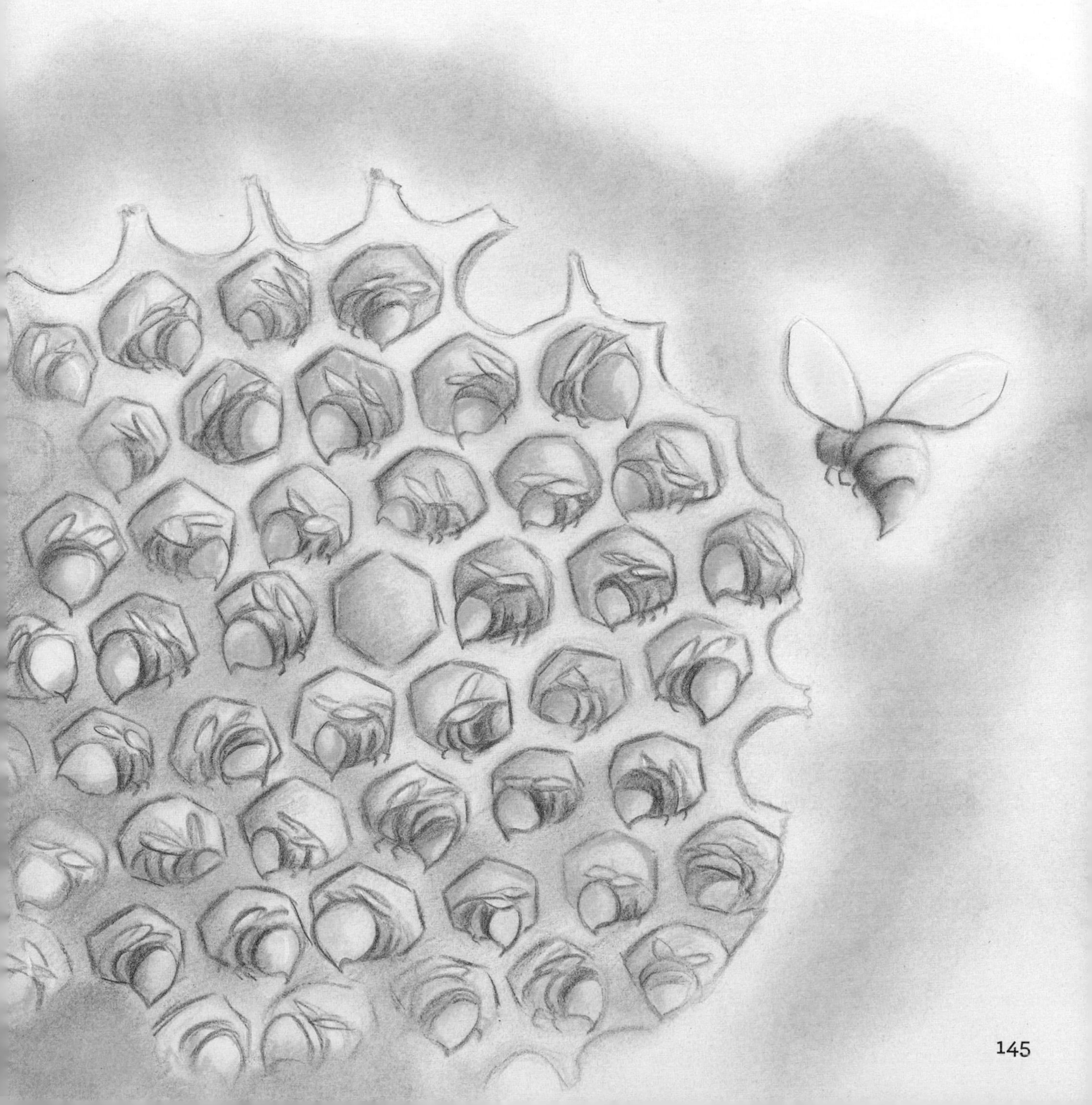

and squirrels lay curled
on heaps of nuts
in hollow trees,

he scratches his big brown bear behind
on the roughest tree trunk he can find,

and old big as a boulder bear
crawls deep into his cave.
He settles his big bear body down,
all covered up
by his bearskin coat,

all wrapped up
in his big hairy bearskin coat,

except

for his no-hair nose.

A very hairy bear
DOES care
about ice cold air
on his no-hair nose,

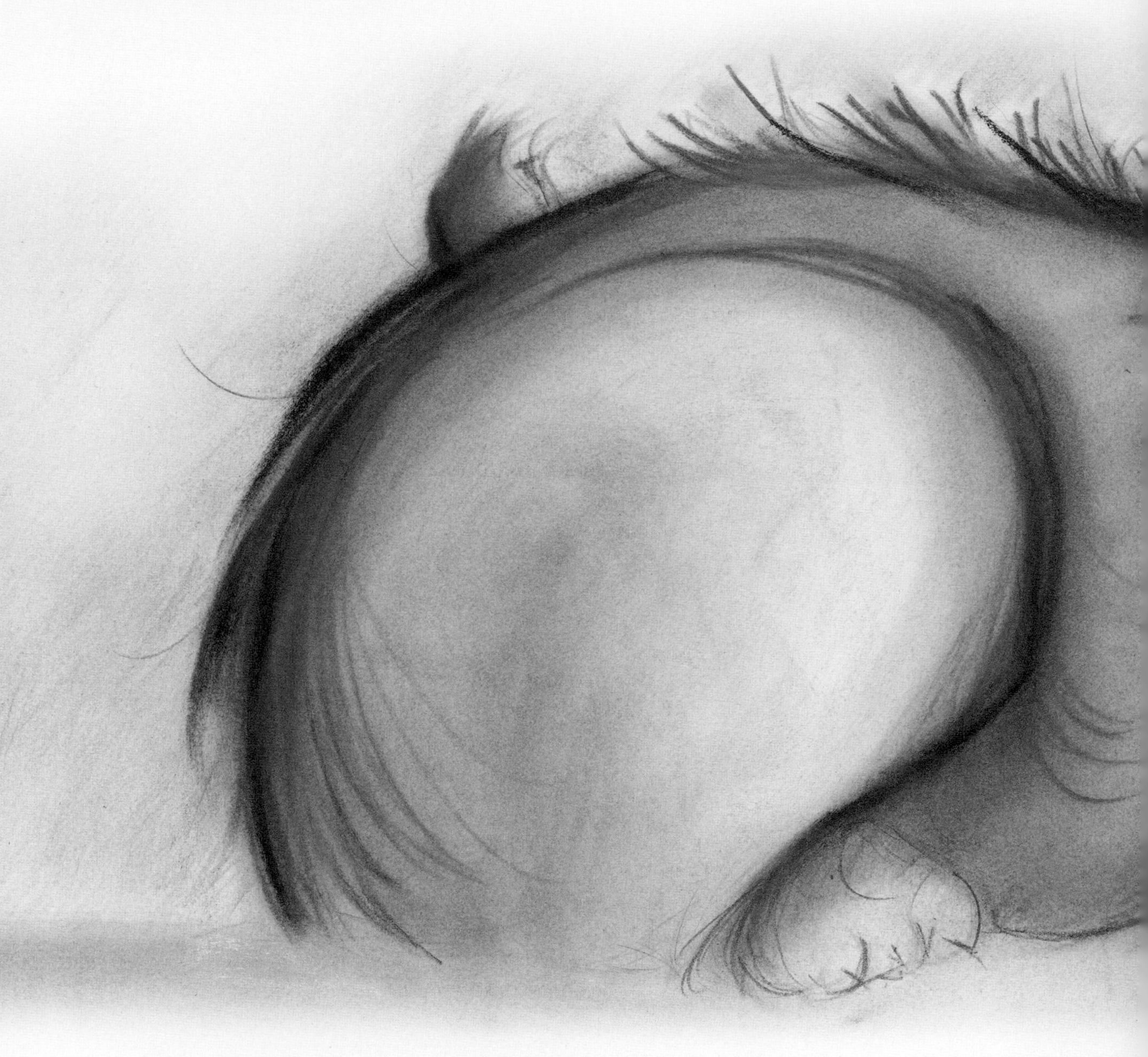

especially

when he's sleepy.

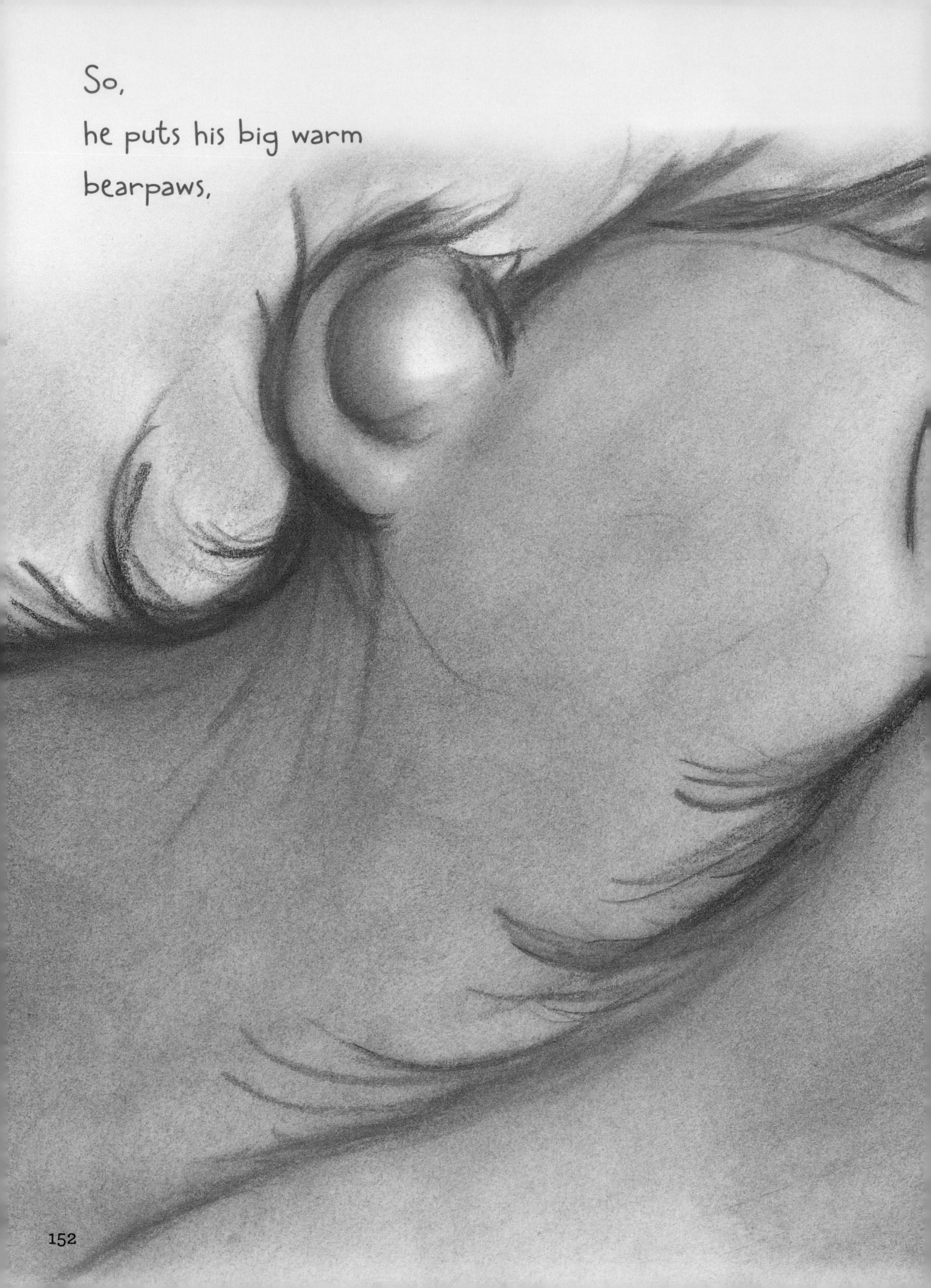

So,

he puts his big warm

bearpaws,

his shaggy, raggy,
very hairy
bearpaws
on top of his nose,

and goes

to sleep.

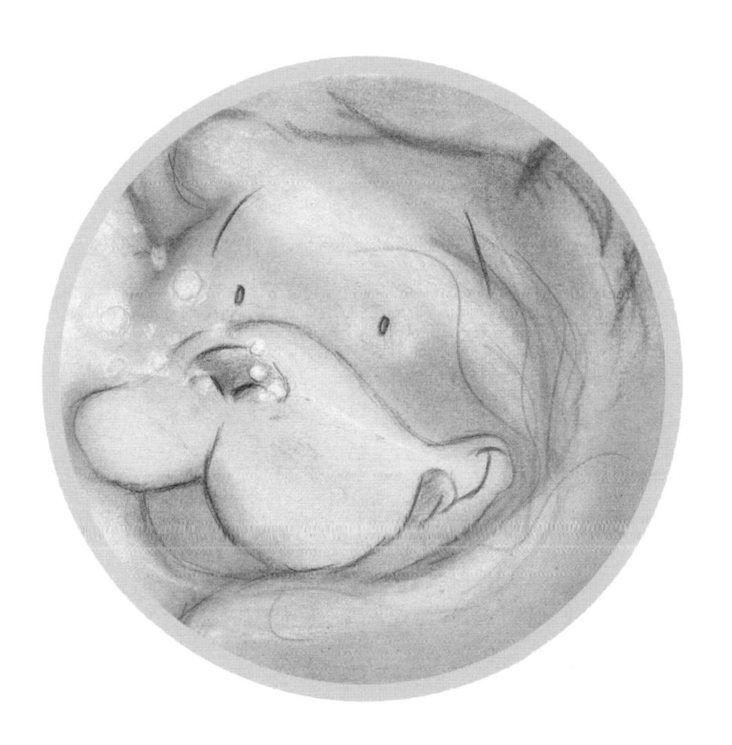

The Dream Jar

by Lindan Lee Johnson

Illustrated by
Serena Curmi

To my parents, Ed and Alice,
for always supporting my dreams, and my daughters, Susannah and Mandalyn, for sharing their own dreams with me
–L.L.J.

To my mum, my dad, and Matt
for always being
proud of me
–S.C.

My sister and I share a sky-blue room at the very tip top of the stairs.

My bed is on the left.
Her bed is on the right.

Our ceiling is covered with stars.

Every night Mom comes up to our room and we take turns reading a story.

She tucks us in,
gives us a snuggle,
turns down the light,
and kisses us good night.

This is the way bedtime is SUPPOSED to be. But some nights it is not. Some nights I have bad dreams and my sister has to save me.

Because sometimes when NIGHT comes, my dreams TURN REAL . . .

My bed is in the middle of the ocean!

SEA MONSTERS

surround me!

My bear falls overboard!

HELP! HELP!

YIKES!

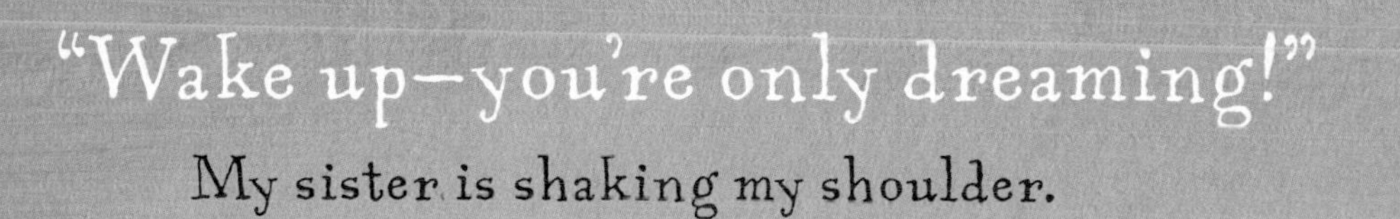

"Wake up—you're only dreaming!"

My sister is shaking my shoulder.

"But it was SOOOO real!"

"Tell me about your dream," my sister says, and listens to every scary word.

Then she lowers her voice.

"I think it's time to tell you

The Secret."

The Secret?

I **LOVE** secrets!

"Mom told me this secret when I was your age. You can change the story of your dreams if you practice. Even if it starts out to be a bad dream, you can make it into a good one . . . a Dreamy Dream."

THIS is very hard to believe.

"Let's start with your bad dream. It was about sea monsters—"
"VERY SCARY SEA MONSTERS!"

"But sea monsters are not real," my sister says. "They are IMAGINARY. So IMAGINE a sea monster that isn't very scary."

"All right, I'll try.
Maybe if the sea monster was *really silly* it wouldn't be SO scary," I say.

"You're right," says my sister. "Now close your eyes and see the really silly sea monsters in your mind. Make up a story about them. Turn your bad dream into a good one . . . a *Dreamy Dream*."
This might just work.

My bed is in the
middle of the ocean,
surrounded by SILLY sea monsters!

Why, this silly sea monster's friendly. He wants to play. I jump from my bed and hop on, and the race to the waves begins!

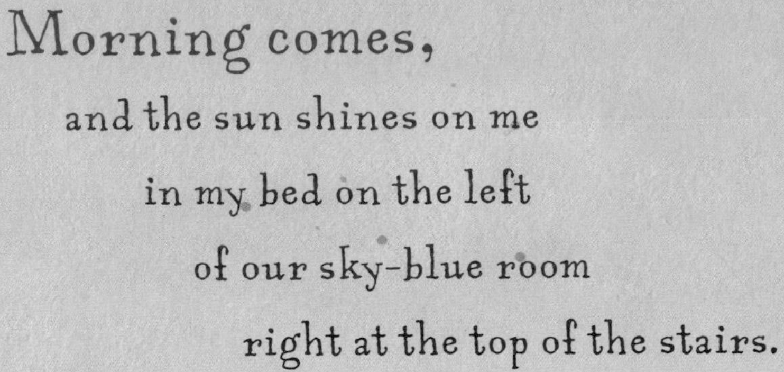

Morning comes,
and the sun shines on me
in my bed on the left
of our sky-blue room
right at the top of the stairs.

It Worked!

My sister knows the secret
of Dreamy Dreams,
and she's always here
to save me.

Until . . .

my sister is invited to a SLEEPOVER.

"You can't go," I tell her. "You need to be here to save me from BAD DREAMS."

"I have an idea," my sister says. "Let's make a list of things that make us laugh or feel good. Things we like to spend a long time thinking about."

"Tonight, you'll find the answer to your dreams,"
my sister tells me.

"Look for it
when the lights
go off."

She smiles her most MYSTERIOUS smile.

That was hours ago.
Finally it's my bedtime.

"Look on the nightstand," my mother says.

There on the nightstand next to the Laughing Moon lamp is a plain jar covered in dark blue paper. I stare at the plain jar on the nightstand. I frown at the plain jar on the night-stand.

"Things are not always what they APPEAR to be,"

my mother says

as she turns down the light.

Suddenly stars *glow up* on the
dark blue paper.
It takes my breath away.
"Your sister left you a note." It says:
Mom smiles.
She must be remembering.

This is The Dream Jar
I made for you—
just like the one Mom
made for me!

When you are having a bad dream, The Dream Jar gives you the power to wake yourself up. Reach inside and take out one Dreamy Dream. Your mind will fill up with happy thoughts. Then you can change the BAD DREAM into a good one.

The Dream Jar
is magic.
I can feel it.

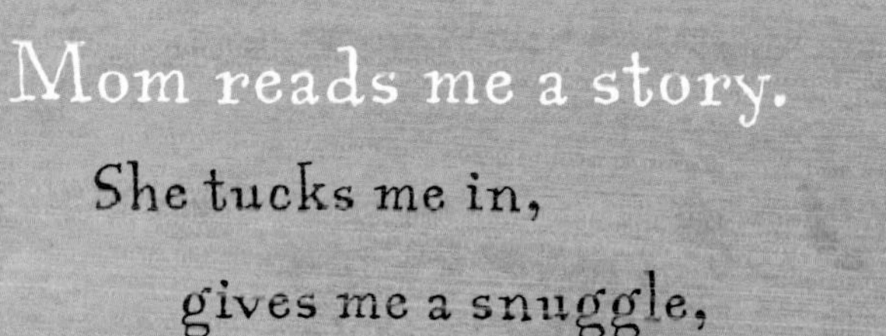

Mom reads me a story.

She tucks me in,

gives me a snuggle,

turns down the light,

and kisses me good night.

"But, Mom, I can't sleep by myself. The terribly horrible dreams will get me!"

"No, they won't," she says. "Your sister gave you The Dream Jar. You will know what to do."

I'm in a dark, scary shopping mall. All the lights in the stores are blinking on and off!

I AM LOST!

Here is the escalator –
I want to go home.

"Wake up—you're only dreaming," I hear my sister's voice say. "Look inside *The Dream Jar!*"

I open one eye, but my sister isn't here.
Then I see The Dream Jar.

I take out one
Dreamy Dream.

I untie the blue string and carefully unroll the little piece of paper. I read the tiny words my sister wrote just for me:

You have a
MAGIC WAND
— use it!

I smile and
close my eyes.

I am back in the shopping mall.

I point my MAGIC WAND
at the chomping escalators and they melt into
slippery, silvery slides that magically go
up and down and ALL AROUND!

On one of the slides,
I see my sister. She laughs and waves at me.
"CONGRATULATIONS!
This is a fabulously FUN
Dreamy Dream!"
It IS a fabulously fun Dreamy Dream. I wave back, and
we share a just-between-sisters smile. Then we soar off
on double loop-de-loops on the slides shining with stars.

And when morning comes,
the sun shines on me
in my bed on the left
of our sky-blue room
right at the top
of the stairs.

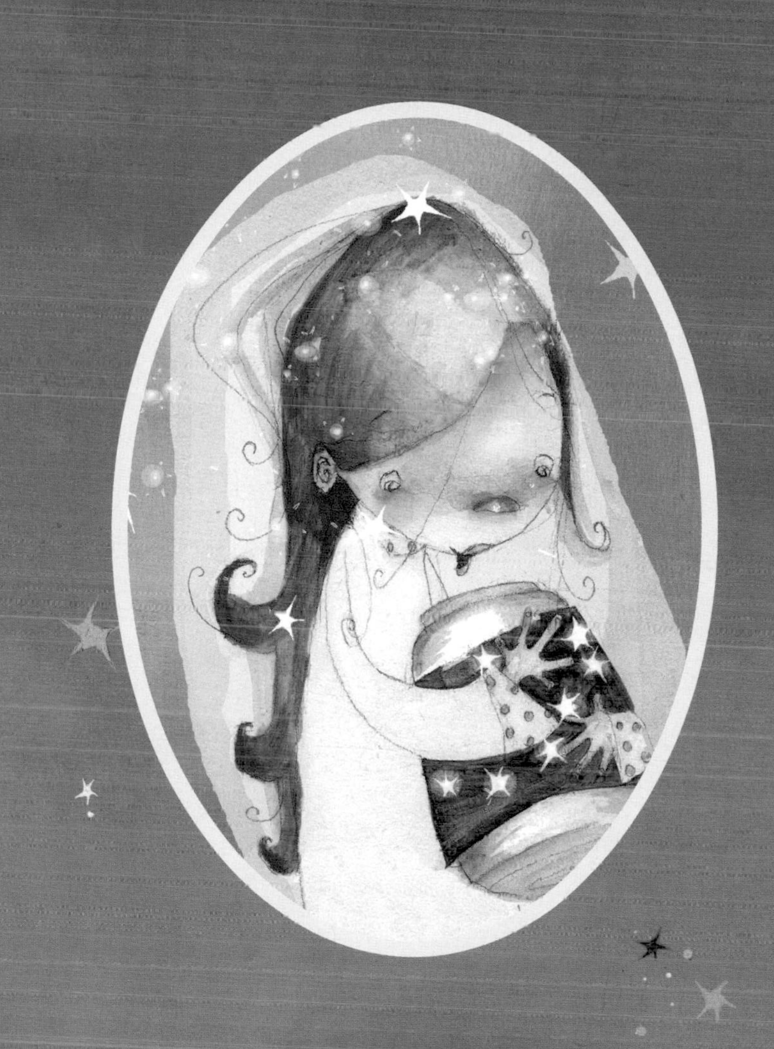

KERRY ARQUETTE

What Did You Do Today?

Illustrated by NANCY HAYASHI

To Mother, who said, "You can."
So I could and I did.
—K.A.

To David and Helen
—N.H.

What did you do today, little dog?
What did you do today?

I wagged my tail and broke a cup.
I tumbled with a neighbor pup.
I chewed my master's slipper up.
That's what I did today.

What did you do today, little cat?
What did you do today?

I rolled in grass and got a burr.
I licked and licked my lovely fur.
I tried to teach the dog to purr.
That's what I did today.

What did you do today, little pig?
What did you do today?

I found some mucky, muddy ground.
I wallowed deep and rolled around.
I made my favorite grunting sound.
That's what I did today.

What did you do today, little chick?
What did you do today?

I watched the grunting pigs get slopped.
I pecked and peeped and hipped and hopped.
I snatched the crumbs the farmer dropped.
That's what I did today.

What did you do today, little bee?
What did you do today?

A brown bear took my honey out.
I buzzed and bumbled all about.
And then I stung him on the snout.
That's what I did today.

What did you do today, little bear?
What did you do today?

I climbed up where the honey grows.
I got a bee sting on my nose.
Oh well, that's how it sometimes goes!
That's what I did today.

What did you do today, little bird?
What did you do today?

My mother taught me how to fly,
To flap and glide across the sky.
The world looks small when I'm so high!
That's what I did today.

What did you do today, little owl?
What did you do today?

While others frolicked in the sun,
I slept until the day was done.
Tonight I'll go to have *my* fun!
That's what I did today.

What did you do today, little child?
What did you do today?

I climbed a tree and flew a kite.
I ran and jumped with all my might.
I bathed and brushed and curled up tight.
Then told the golden moon,
"Good night."

That's what I did today.

Fair

Piggies

WRITTEN BY
DON AND AUDREY WOOD

ILLUSTRATED BY
DON WOOD

Dedicated to Marjane Wood

I've got two fat little piggies,

two smart little piggies,

P

two long little piggies,

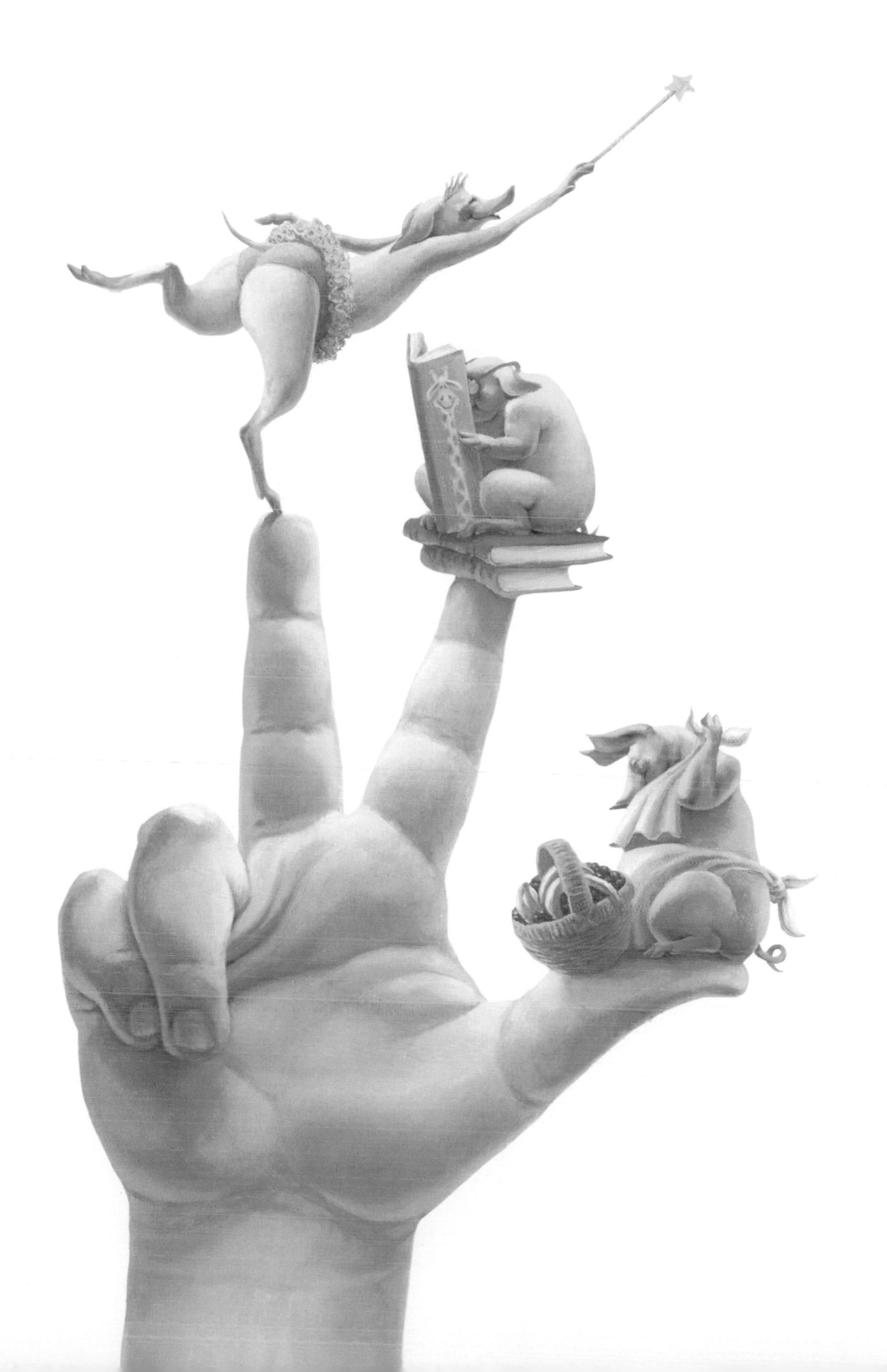

two silly little piggies,

and two wee

little piggies.

Sometimes they're
hot little piggies,

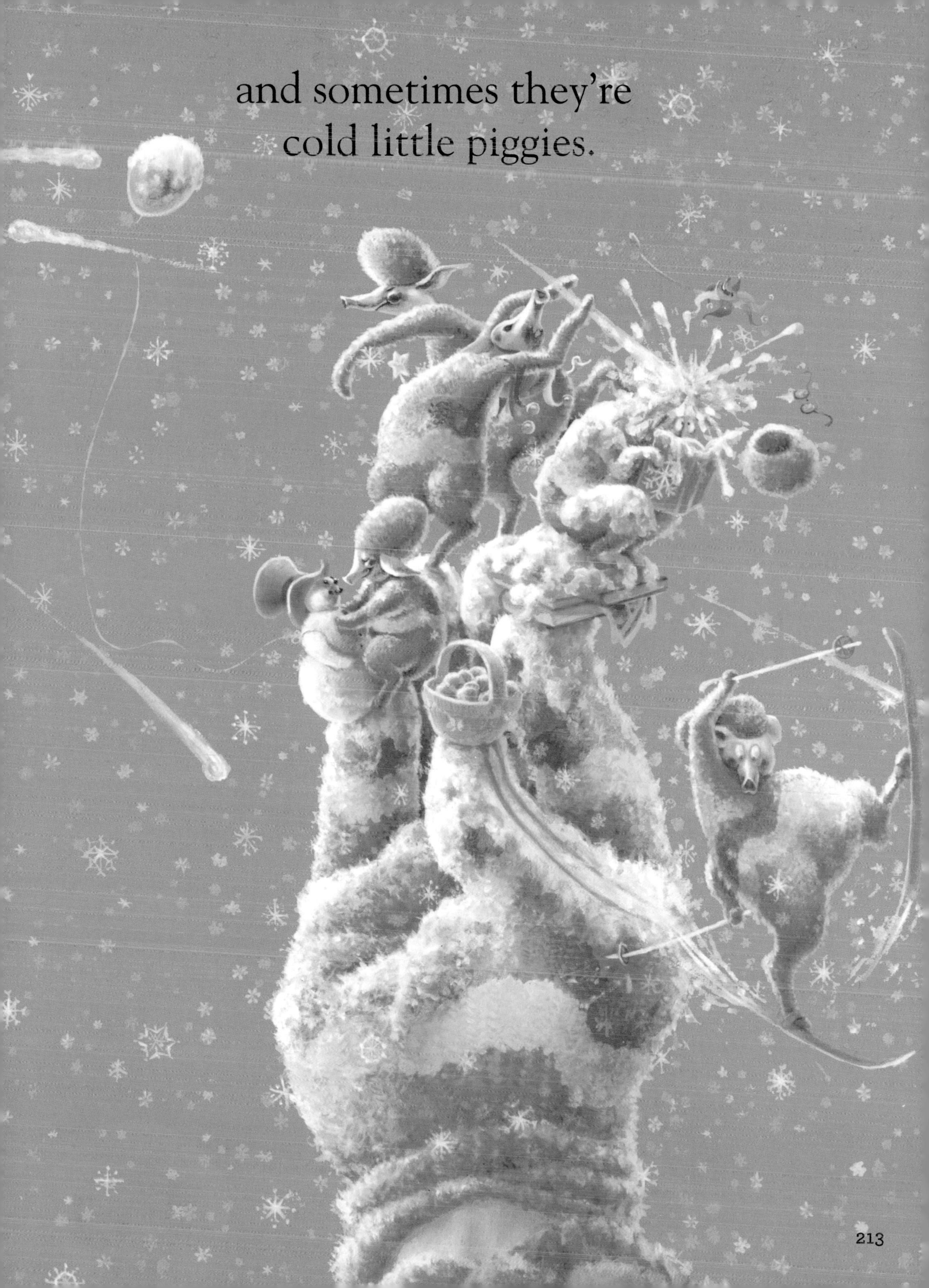

and sometimes they're
cold little piggies.

Sometimes they're
clean little piggies,

and sometimes they're
dirty little piggies.

Sometimes they're

good little piggies,

but not at bedtime.

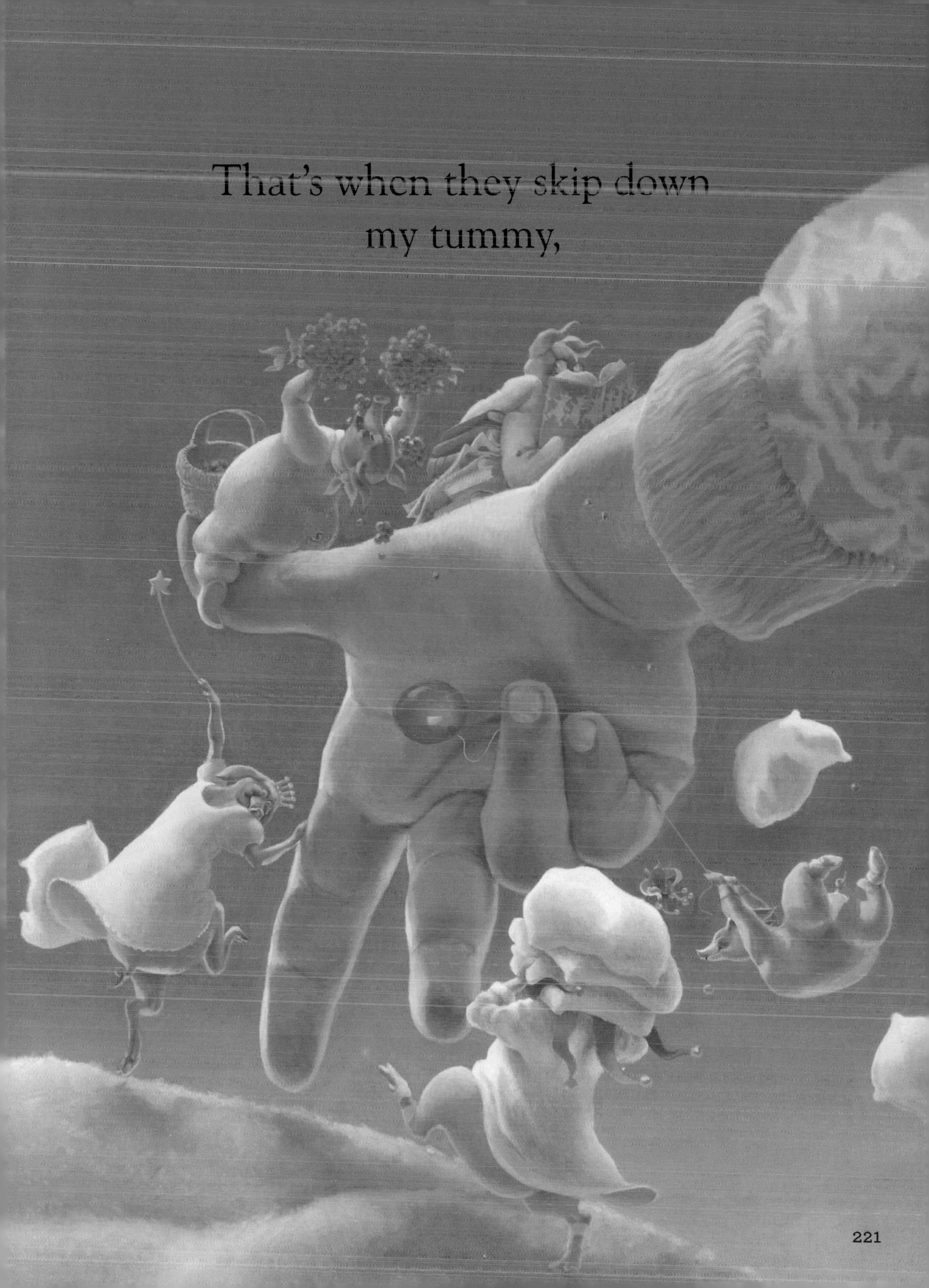

That's when they skip down
my tummy,

dance on my toes,

then run away and hide.

So . . .

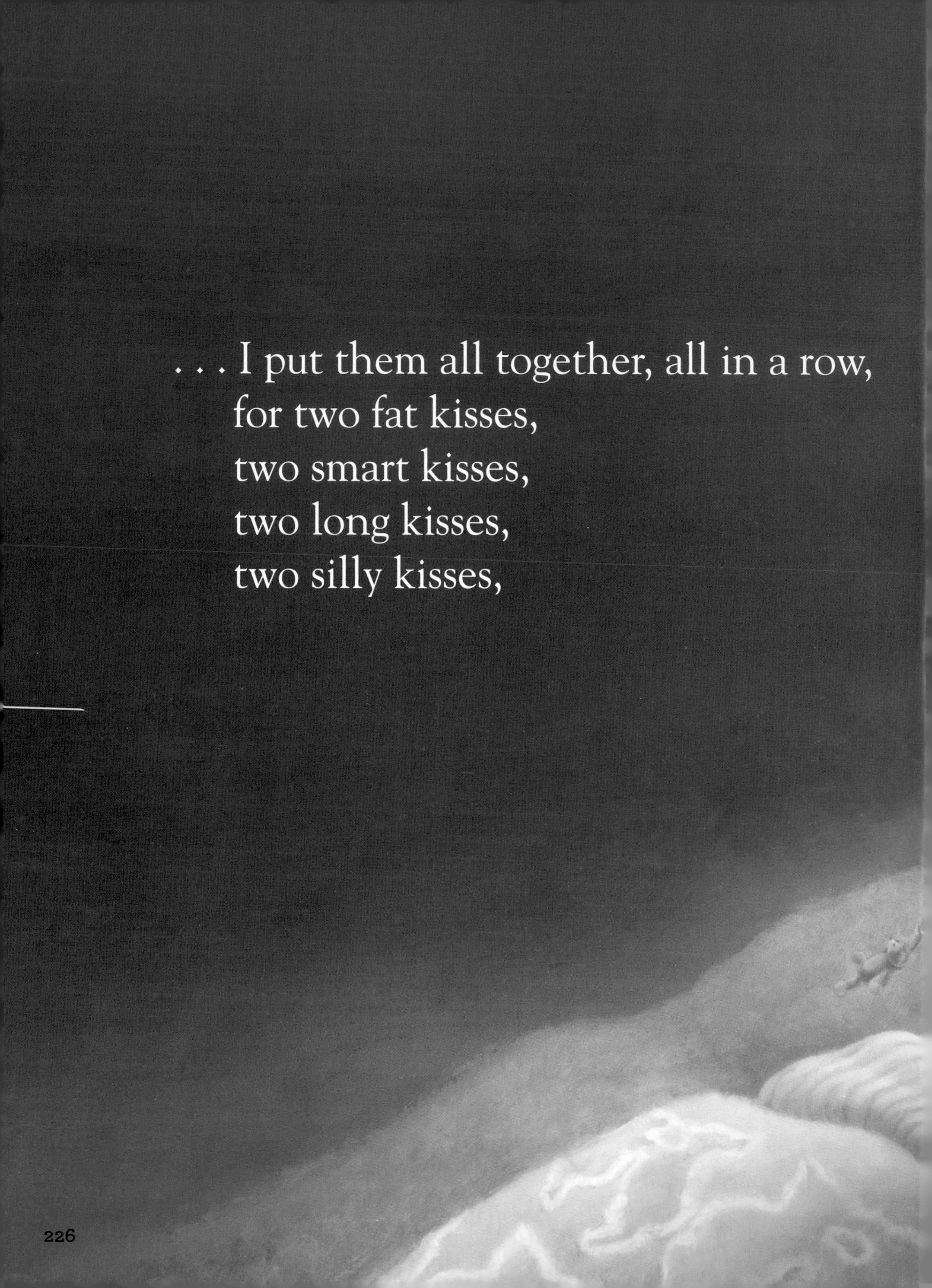

. . . I put them all together, all in a row,
for two fat kisses,
two smart kisses,
two long kisses,
two silly kisses,

and two wee kisses goodnight.

About the Authors and Illustrators

H. A. REY and **MARGRET REY** escaped Nazi-occupied Paris in 1940 by bicycle, carrying the manuscript for the first book about Curious George. They came to live in the United States, and *Curious George* was published in 1941. You can learn more about the Reys and Curious George and access games, activities, and more at www.curiousgeorge.com.

CECE MENG is a school volunteer, Girl Scout leader, and gymnastics mom. She lives with her husband and their two children, a bird named Lulu, and three spotted rabbits in Santa Cruz, California. Visit her website at www.cecemeng.com.

JOY ANG is an illustrator who has worked in both the comic and gaming industries. She lives in Edmonton, Canada, and is one of the editors/creators of a comic anthology called *The Anthology Project.* Some of her most recent children's books include *Mustache Baby* (by Bridget Heos) and *Hullabaloo* (by Ammi-Joan Paquette). You can visit her website at www.joyang.ca.

NATASHA WING is the author of more than twenty books for children, including the best-selling series The Night Before . . . She lives in Fort Collins, Colorado, with her husband and very sleepy cat. Visit www.natashawing.com.

SYLVIE KANTOROVITZ has illustrated several picture books under the name Sylvie Wickstrom, as well as her own *The Very Tiny Baby* and the popular Little Witch easy reader series. She lives in Albany, New York.

JOANNE RYDER is the author of many books for children, including *Won't You Be My Kissaroo?* illustrated by Melissa Sweet, *Each Living Thing* illustrated by Ashley Wolff, *The Snail's Spell,* and *Earthdance.* She lives in Pacific Grove, California.

MELISSA SWEET has illustrated numerous picture books including her own *Balloons over Broadway* and *Welcome, Baby!: Baby Rhymes for Baby Times* by Stephanie Calmenson. Her vivid illustrations have won a Caldecott Honor and two New York Times Best Illustrated citations. She lives in Rockport, Maine. Visit her website at www.melissasweet.net.

Charlotte Jane Battles Bedtime is **MYRA WOLFE**'s debut picture book. She lives in Portland, Oregon, with her family.

MARIA MONESCILLO has worked as an animator and children's book illustrator in her native Spain. She now lives in Norway with her husband and daughters.

MARGOT APPLE has illustrated more than fifty books for children, including *Sheep in a Jeep, Big Mama,* and *Just Like My Dad.* Her own best loved are *Blanket* and *Brave Martha,* which she wrote as well as illustrated. Her work has also appeared in *Country Journal* and *Ladybug* magazines. Margot lives in Shelburne Falls, Massachusetts, with her husband, horses, and a number of cats.

ALICE SCHERTLE is the author of *Little Blue Truck, Little Blue Truck Leads the Way,* and many other well-loved books for children, including *All You Need for a Snowman.* She lives in Plainfield, Massachusetts.

MATT PHELAN's many books include *The Storm in the Barn,* winner of the Scott O'Dell Award. He lives in Philadelphia. Visit him at www.mattphelan.com.

LINDAN LEE JOHNSON is a graduate of the Vermont College MFA in Writing for Children program. She has four cats, three brothers, two daughters, and one house near Dallas, Texas.

SERENA CURMI grew up on a sailboat and traveled with her family in the United States, Europe, and places in between. Serena illustrates children's books, and also greeting cards and magazines. She currently resides in Bristol, England. Visit her website at www.serenacurmiillustration.com.

What Did You Do Today? is **KERRY ARQUETTE**'s first children's book. She lives in Denver, Colorado.

NANCY HAYASHI is the illustrator of *Bunny Bungalow* by Cynthia Rylant, *I Can Do It Myself!* by Diane Adams, and *Raymond and Nelda* by Barbara Bottner. She lives in Los Angeles, California.

DON WOOD and **AUDREY WOOD** are the husband-and-wife creators of many beloved books for children, including *The Napping House, Heckedy Peg,* and *King Bidgood's in the Bathtub,* a Caldecott Honor book. The Woods live in Hawaii. www.audreywood.com.

www.hmhco.com
ISBN 978-0-544-30178-8

Designed by Carol Chu & Kayleigh McCann

Houghton Mifflin Harcourt Publishing Company
222 Berkeley Street
Boston, Massachusetts 02116

Manufactured in China
SCP 10 9 8 7 6 5 4 3 2 1
4500461128